SEEDS OF CHANGE

GREGORY REICHMUTH

MASTERING THE CLASSROOM
Always Teach-Up!

CONTENTS

AUTHOR BIO:

GREGORY REICHMUTH

Gregory Reichmuth is a passionate and dedicated educational leader with over 20 years of experience in the field. He currently teaches in the Engineering & Programming Department at STEM School in Highlands Ranch, Colorado. Gregory has also served as a teacher in Denver Public Schools, where he was recognized for his commitment to accountability and educational excellence while working in their Alternative Educational Program.

Dr. Rodney Blunck, a respected Associate Clinical Professor at the University of Colorado Denver, describes Gregory as "one of the most passionate and accountability-oriented educational leaders" he has ever worked with. Gregory is known for his action-oriented leadership, his ability to challenge the status quo, and his unwavering commitment to social justice and public education. He excels in promoting cohesion among staff, developing a collective purpose, and advocating for students, families, and communities.

Gregory's leadership style is characterized by integrity, effective communication, and a collaborative nature. He is a visionary who inspires others with his energy and enthusiasm, consistently working to improve the lives of those in the educational community. As Dr. Blunck notes, Gregory "models leadership, sets clear goals and objectives, and has high expectations for colleagues and staff."

In addition to his professional accomplishments, Gregory is deeply committed to fostering a world-class educational environment. He dedicates countless hours to working on behalf of children, parents, and communities, always striving to put his beliefs and vision into practice. Gregory Reichmuth's dedication to education and his ability to lead with hope and integrity make him a valuable asset to any educational organization. His work continues to inspire and influence educators and students alike.

DEDICATION

To my beloved mother, Barbara Ann Reichmuth
(1941 - 2024).

Your unwavering love, wisdom, and inspiration have shaped the person I am today. Your strength, kindness, and dedication to our family and your endless encouragement to pursue my dreams will forever be remembered and cherished.

This book series is dedicated to you, Mom. Your spirit lives on in every word, and your legacy of inspiration continues to guide me. Thank you for being my guiding light and my greatest supporter. I love you and miss you every day.

In loving memory,
Gregory Reichmuth

INTRODUCTION

In the quiet solitude of a dimly lit room lined with shelves of well-worn books, Margaret sat at an antique wooden desk, her hands gently riffling through a stack of black-and-white photographs. Each one was a portal to a past that seemed both distant and vividly present. The window beside her framed a view of modern Chicago, its towering skyscrapers bathed in the golden hues of sunset, but inside her study, the world was as it had been decades ago.

The photographs spilled across the desk like leaves scattered by an autumn wind. Here was a class of 1934, the children's faces round and serious, posed in front of the old brick schoolhouse on Halsted Street, now just a memory replaced by a parking lot. There, a candid shot of a school play, makeshift costumes, and painted cardboard sets, a testament to the creativity that scarcity had necessitated and inspired.

Margaret's fingers paused on a particular photograph, her touch tender, almost reverent. It was a simple picture: a young boy, Jimmy Doyle, stood at the forefront, his smile bright and wide, a stark contrast to the patched elbows of his sweater. Behind him, his classmates stood in two uneven rows, their expressions a mixture of resilience and youthful optimism. This photo, more than others, tugged at her heartstrings.

She leaned back in her chair, her eyes drifting from the photograph to the window, watching as the present-day city flickered to life with the onset of evening. The streets below were filled with the hum of traffic and the rush of people, each absorbed in their own lives, unaware of the gaze of the woman who had once molded the minds of their predecessors.

Margaret's mind wandered back to those days when the Great Depression cast a long, somber shadow over the city. The challenges had been immense, not just academically but emotionally and morally. How had she managed? It was more than just teaching arithmetic or spelling; it was instilling hope, weaving a tapestry of community and resilience when the fabric of society seemed threadbare.

Her reverie was broken by the soft chime of the clock on the mantle, marking the hour. Time had moved inexorably forward, and yet, within these four walls, it looped back on itself, replaying the moments captured in black and white, echoing the laughter and whispers of children long grown.

Margaret picked up the photograph again, her decision made. It was time those stories were told, the lessons shared not just in memories but in words. She would write it all down, the testament of a time when change was wrought not by the mighty or the wealthy, but by the young and the brave, guided by one who believed in the transformative power of education.

With a deep breath, she opened the top drawer of her desk, pulling out a fresh notebook and a pen, the tools of her trade that had never failed her. As she turned to the first blank page, the photograph beside her, Margaret felt the years slip away, the weight of them both a burden and a blessing. The story would begin with Jimmy, a boy with a bright smile and patched elbows, who epitomized all that had been and all that could be. In telling his story, she would tell the story of many, planting the seeds of change anew.

CHAPTER 1

JIMMY'S STRUGGLES

As the crisp autumn air nipped at Jimmy's cheeks, he lingered at the edge of the bustling schoolyard, his eyes cast downward at the worn soles of his shoes—one toe poking awkwardly through a frayed hole. He tugged at his sweater, the elbows patched with mismatched fabric from an old dress his mother had found. The disparity between his attire and that of his peers was stark; his clothes whispered tales of hardship louder than any words ever could.

Around him, the air was filled with the carefree laughter of his classmates, their joy forming a melody that seemed to belong to another universe. They tossed a ball back and forth, their movements fluid and unburdened by the weight he felt on his own shoulders. There was a time when Jimmy would have been right in the mix, slinging the old apple around with the best of them, but now, the fear of being ribbed for his tattered threads kept him glued to his spot.

Margaret, observing from her vantage point by the classroom door, noted Jimmy's hesitation. With a gentle stride, she approached him, her presence reassuring yet unobtrusive. The backdrop of the school—a sturdy brick building that had been one of the few constants through the trying years of the Great Depression—seemed to contrast with the fleeting changes happening all around. **ROOSEVELT'S NEW DEAL PROGRAMS WERE JUST BEGINNING TO EASE THE STRAIN, BUT MANY FAMILIES, INCLUDING JIMMY'S, WERE STILL STRUGGLING TO GET BY.** The **WORKS PROGRESS ADMINISTRATION (WPA)** had brought much-needed jobs to the city, with men repairing streets and building public facilities, yet these programs hadn't reached every household.

"Jimmy," she called out softly, making sure her voice conveyed comfort rather than concern.

He looked up, his smile a fragile mask over his unease. "Mornin', Miss Margaret," he murmured, clutching his books close to his chest as if they might shield him from the scrutiny he feared.

"Ready to hit the books?" Margaret asked, her tone light but her eyes keen, reading the subtle language of his discomfort. **MARGARET HAD SPENT HER CAREER INSPIRED BY THE LIKES OF JANE ADDAMS**, the social reformer and advocate who had founded Hull House not far from here. **MARGARET BELIEVED, AS ADDAMS DID, IN THE TRANSFORMATIVE POWER OF EDUCATION, PARTICULARLY FOR THE CHILDREN OF IMMIGRANTS AND BLACK FAMILIES WHO HAD COME TO CHICAGO DURING THE GREAT MIGRATION, SEARCHING FOR A BETTER LIFE.**

JIMMY WAS NOT THE ONLY ONE IN HIS CLASS WHOSE FAMILY HAD FACED STRUGGLE. The class was a mix of children, some from Irish and Polish backgrounds like Jimmy, and others whose families had moved north from the segregated South. Margaret had seen firsthand how families—Black and white—arrived in Chicago hoping for better opportunities, only to be met with poverty, poor working conditions, and, for Black families, discrimination that followed them from the South. She knew the weight that students like Jimmy carried on their young shoulders.

"Yeah, I'm all set," Jimmy replied, though his voice lacked its usual pep. He managed a nod, though his gaze quickly flicked away, landing on anything but her probing, kind eyes.

Margaret placed a comforting hand on his shoulder. "There's a nip in the air today, isn't there? Let's head on inside. I've rustled up something special for us today," she suggested, her words wrapped in the warmth of routine and learning.

As they walked towards the classroom, the distant hum of a radio broadcast drifted from an open window nearby—President Roosevelt's voice crackled through the air, delivering one of his famous **FIRESIDE CHATS**. "We have nothing to fear but fear itself," he declared, as hopeful as ever, though the streets of Chicago told a different story. **FOR FAMILIES LIKE JIMMY'S, AND THE BLACK FAMILIES CROWDED INTO CHICAGO'S SOUTH SIDE, HOPE WAS SOMETIMES HARD TO COME BY, DESPITE ROOSEVELT'S ASSURANCES.**

Inside, the classroom was a sanctuary from the biting wind, the air redolent with the familiar scents of old books and chalk dust. On one wall, a map of the United States hung, with notes about the **CIVILIAN CONSERVATION CORPS (CCC)** and **WPA** projects dotted across the Midwest, reminders of the ways in which the country was rebuilding itself, piece by piece. Margaret ushered Jimmy to his usual seat at the front—not just to keep him engaged but to keep a close watch over him. She had noticed a change in him; the bright spark that once lit his eyes now seemed dimmer, veiled with worry.

As the other students streamed in, their voices filled the room, starkly contrasting with Jimmy's silence. He pulled out his well-worn notebook, the cover creased and the pages nearly full. A quick glance around confirmed his fears; his gear was as battered as his spirits, while his mates' kit looked fresh off the rack. He shrank lower in his seat, hoping to blend into the background.

Margaret kicked off the class with a warm-up exercise that had everyone buzzing, but her thoughts remained partly on Jimmy. She pieced together the signs of his distress, her resolve firming with each passing moment. By the end of the day, she was determined to find a way to help him, to rekindle the vibrant, enthusiastic student she knew still burned beneath the ashes of adversity.

As she began to outline the day's lesson, Margaret referenced a recent headline from the Chicago Tribune, "**FDR DECLARES BANK HOLIDAY TO STABILIZE ECONOMY**." The students listened intently, curious about how these national events affected their lives. Margaret used moments like this to connect the world outside to their own struggles, reminding them that the winds of change didn't just blow through the halls of Washington, D.C., but also swept through their very streets.

"Can anyone tell me what the New Deal is?" she asked, her eyes sweeping across the room. "What does it mean for us, here in Chicago?"

Hands slowly rose, tentative at first. **ANNA, ONE OF THE BRIGHTEST STUDENTS IN THE CLASS, AND ONE OF MANY GIRLS WHO HAD STEPPED INTO ROLES OF RESPONSIBILITY WHILE THEIR BROTHERS AND FATHERS WERE AWAY, VENTURED A GUESS.**

"It's the government trying to help us, right? Like… the CCC? My brother's working with them up in Wisconsin. He sends money back to us."

Jimmy listened, his heart tightening. He had no older brother to send money, no WPA job to lift his family out of the mire. But he clung to the idea that things could change—that perhaps, as President Roosevelt promised, better days were coming. If not for them now, then someday soon.

AS Margaret continued to teach, the day's lesson—both in the textbook and in life—was one of perseverance, of community, and of the strength found in even the most trying times. **OUTSIDE, CHICAGO'S TOWERING SKYLINE, STILL DOTTED WITH WPA CONSTRUCTION SITES, STOOD AS A TESTAMENT TO THE CITY'S RESILIENCE**—a resilience reflected in every worn notebook and patched sweater within her classroom.

CHAPTER 2

RIPPLES OF CHANGE

The school bell rang, slicing through the morning hustle as kids swarmed into the classroom, their laughter and chatter filling the air with a youthful vibrance. Yet amidst the typical morning commotion, a quiet undercurrent of whispers flowed as eyes darted toward Jimmy Doyle. Each day, his clothes seemed more worn, his shoulders more hunched under the invisible weight he carried. **THE DISPARITY BETWEEN HIS PATCHED-UP TROUSERS AND THE NEWER JEANS OF HIS CLASSMATES WAS STARK, PAINTING A PICTURE OF A BOY SLOWLY DRIFTING TO THE OUTSKIRTS OF HIS PEER CIRCLE.** The effects of the Great Depression had not yet loosened their grip on the city. For families like Jimmy's, recovery was a distant dream, despite **PRESIDENT ROOSEVELT'S BOLD PROMISES ON THE RADIO** and the sweeping changes of the **NEW DEAL.**

Anna, a sharp-eyed girl with a kind heart, noticed more than just the frayed fabrics and faded colors of Jimmy's attire. She saw the subtle withdrawal in his smile, the slow retreat in his engagement. **HER FATHER OFTEN READ ALOUD FROM THE CHICAGO TRIBUNE AT THE DINNER TABLE, RECOUNTING STORIES OF FAMILIES LOSING HOMES AND LIVELIHOODS, WHILE ROOSEVELT PUSHED FORWARD WITH NEW DEAL PROGRAMS.** But for families like Jimmy's, the changes hadn't yet arrived at their doorstep. **THE GAP BETWEEN ROOSEVELT'S OPTIMISM AND THE GRIM REALITY FOR WORKING-CLASS FAMILIES WAS BECOMING MORE OBVIOUS, AND JIMMY'S QUIET DEMEANOR REFLECTED THAT DISSONANCE.** As they settled into their seats, Anna's resolve hardened. Today, she would bridge the gap that discomfort and uncertainty had widened.

Lunchtime brought the usual clamor of voices and the clatter of lunchboxes on the cafeteria tables. Anna unwrapped her sandwich, a generous extra helping of turkey tucked between the bread—her mother always packed too much, she claimed, but perhaps there was an intention behind the abundance. **HER FAMILY WAS FORTUNATE; HER FATHER HAD FOUND WORK WITH THE WPA, HELPING TO BUILD THE VERY ROADS THEY WALKED ON TO GET TO SCHOOL.** But Anna knew not everyone in their class had been so lucky. Glancing over at Jimmy, who fumbled with a small, somewhat crushed apple, Anna slid over to his table.

"Hey, Jimmy," she greeted with a cheerfulness she hoped was contagious. "You look like you could use a bit more than that. Care for half of my sandwich? Ma's convinced I'm still growing enough to eat two of everything."

Jimmy looked up, surprise flickering across his features before a cautious relief took its place. "That's mighty keen of you, Anna. Thanks," he murmured, accepting the sandwich half. The other kids at the table watched, the air tingling with a mix of curiosity and newfound understanding. In a time when people were learning to make do with less, such acts of sharing carried weight. **THEY REFLECTED A COLLECTIVE RESILIENCE THAT HAD SPROUTED IN COMMUNITIES ACROSS THE COUNTRY, WHERE NEIGHBORS HELPED NEIGHBORS JUST TO SURVIVE.** Even in their young lives, these students were beginning to understand the importance of mutual aid.

This small act seemed to thaw the chill that had begun to settle around Jimmy. **THE OTHER STUDENTS, TAKING THEIR CUE FROM ANNA, SLOWLY STARTED ENGAGING HIM MORE OPENLY**, asking questions about the latest baseball game and even chuckling at his dry quips about the players' performances. Jimmy's responses grew less guarded, a soft warmth returning to his voice as the meal continued.

Inspired by Anna's example, others began to extend small gestures of kindness toward Jimmy. **MICHAEL OFFERED TO SHARE HIS NOTES FROM THE HISTORY CLASS JIMMY HAD MISSED LAST WEEK. THEY HAD BEEN LEARNING ABOUT THE CIVILIAN CONSERVATION CORPS (CCC), A PROGRAM THAT HAD EMPLOYED THOUSANDS OF YOUNG MEN ACROSS THE COUNTRY.** "My older brother's working with the CCC in the north," Michael had said. "He's been sending us a few dollars a month. It's not much, but it's keeping us afloat." **THIS WAS THE REALITY FOR MANY FAMILIES—GOVERNMENT PROGRAMS LIKE THE CCC AND WPA WERE A LIFELINE, THOUGH THEY HADN'T REACHED EVERYONE.** The parallels between their lessons and Jimmy's reality were striking. Clara, noticing Jimmy's worn-out shoes, whispered to her mother that evening about organizing a clothing drive at the school. The word spread, and soon, a quiet campaign of compassion wove its way through their class.

MARGARET OBSERVED THESE CHANGES FROM THE SIDELINES, HER HEART SWELLING WITH A MIX OF PRIDE AND RELIEF. She had long admired Jane Addams' work in Chicago's **HULL HOUSE**, where Addams had created spaces for community and mutual support during tough times. Margaret knew that fostering empathy and understanding among her students was just as important as teaching them math or history. **DURING A PARTICULARLY REFLECTIVE AFTERNOON LESSON, SHE DECIDED TO STEER THE CONVERSATION TOWARDS THE IMPORTANCE OF COMMUNITY AND SUPPORT.**

"Class, today let's talk about something more than just our usual subjects," Margaret began, leaning against the chalkboard with arms gently crossed. "Let's discuss what it means to really be there for each other, especially during tough times like these."

As she spoke, her words seemed to echo the larger national conversation about pulling together as a nation. **ROOSEVELT'S RECENT FIRESIDE CHATS HAD EMPHASIZED THE IMPORTANCE OF COLLECTIVE ACTION AND CIVIC DUTY.** Margaret wanted her students to understand that even at their age, they could make a difference in each other's lives. The discussion that unfolded was vibrant and thoughtful, with students sharing insights and stories about times they had helped or been helped. **ANNA RECOUNTED HOW HER FATHER'S JOB WITH THE WPA HAD HELPED NOT ONLY HER FAMILY BUT ALSO ALLOWED HIM TO CONTRIBUTE TO LOCAL COMMUNITY PROJECTS.**

THE CLASSROOM, USUALLY A PLACE OF ACADEMIC LEARNING, TRANSFORMED INTO A

WARM FORUM FOR SHARING AND EMPATHY, RE-INFORCING THE BONDS THAT WERE QUIETLY STRENGTHENING AROUND THEM. Margaret saw the power of these small moments, understanding that these lessons in kindness would ripple outward, affecting not just the students in her class but the broader community.

As the school day ended, and the students filed out of the classroom, Margaret caught Jimmy's eye and nodded with an unspoken message of encouragement. **JIMMY, FOR THE FIRST TIME IN WEEKS, FELT SEEN—TRULY SEEN—NOT AS A BOY STRUGGLING WITH POVERTY, BUT AS SOMEONE WORTH CARING ABOUT.** Feeling a buoyancy that had been absent for too long, he nodded back, a small smile playing on his lips. The ripples of change, started by a simple act of sharing a sandwich, had begun to reshape the landscape of their classroom, turning it into a place not just of learning, but of understanding and care.

CHAPTER 3

BEYOND THE CLASSROOM WALLS (REVISED)

As autumn deepened into winter, the sharp bite of the cold became a constant reminder of the harsh realities facing many families in Jimmy's neighborhood. The streets of Chicago, already worn by the weight of the Great Depression, were bracing for another brutal season. President Roosevelt's **FIRESIDE CHATS** continued to offer hope, but for families like Jimmy's, the struggle for warmth and food was a daily battle. **MARGARET'S CLASSROOM DISCUSSIONS ABOUT RESILIENCE AND COMMUNITY WERE NOW MORE RELEVANT THAN EVER, AS THE NEW DEAL PROGRAMS SLOWLY TRIED TO BRING RELIEF, THOUGH THEIR REACH WAS LIMITED.** The lessons in Margaret's classroom about **CIVIC RESPONSIBILITY AND MUTUAL AID** were about to transcend the school walls and weave into the fabric of their everyday lives.

One brisk Monday morning, Margaret introduced a new project, her eyes sweeping across her attentive students. "Class, we've talked a lot about what it means to support each other inside these walls," she began, her voice imbued with a gentle firmness. "Now, it's time we take that spirit of community outside, to the streets where we live. We're going to start a neighborhood drive, just like the ones popping up across the country as part of the **COMMUNITY RELIEF EFFORTS ORGANIZED BY THE WPA**. We'll collect food, clothes, whatever necessities people can spare, to help those hit hardest by these tough times."

The classroom buzzed with excited whispers and eager nods. **MARGARET HAD DRAWN INSPIRATION FROM BOTH THE NATIONWIDE EFFORTS OF THE WPA AND LOCAL INITIATIVES, LIKE JANE ADDAMS' HULL HOUSE, WHICH HAD LONG BEEN A BEACON OF COMMUNITY SUPPORT IN CHICAGO.** Her announcement ignited a spark of purpose in her students, giving them a chance to make a tangible difference in the lives of their neighbors. **THEY HAD DISCUSSED ROOSEVELT'S PROGRAMS—SUCH AS THE CIVILIAN CONSERVATION CORPS (CCC)—AND NOW, THEY WOULD TAKE THAT SPIRIT OF SERVICE INTO THEIR OWN COMMUNITY.**

Jimmy felt a surge of energy at the idea. Here was something he could contribute to, something that might even help his own family. He approached Margaret after class, his friends Anna and Michael in tow. "Miss Margaret, we want to help get the drive going. What do we need to do first?"

Margaret smiled, pleased by their enthusiasm. "That's wonderful, Jimmy. First, we need to spread the word. We'll make flyers to hand out and put up around the neighborhood. Anna, you're creative with words—can you write up something catchy? Jimmy, Michael, perhaps you two can help distribute them?"

The trio nodded, diving into their tasks with zeal. **ANNA, WHOSE FATHER HAD RECENTLY FOUND WORK THROUGH THE NEW DEAL PROGRAMS, REFLECTED ON HOW ROOSEVELT'S POLICIES WERE CREATING JOBS AND REBUILDING COMMUNITIES.** But there were still many who fell through the cracks, families like Jimmy's. Her flyer called for unity, referencing Roosevelt's famous words, "We have nothing to fear but fear itself," to inspire their neighbors to act. Jimmy and Michael walked block by block, talking to shop owners and neighbors, explaining the drive and posting flyers in windows and on bulletin boards.

The response was heartening. **PEOPLE WHO HAD FOUND WORK THROUGH THE WPA OR CCC WERE EAGER TO GIVE BACK, RECOGNIZING HOW CLOSE THEY HAD COME TO DESTITUTION THEMSELVES.** Local shopkeepers, many of whom had narrowly avoided closure thanks to **ROOSEVELT'S BANKING REFORMS**, contributed what they could—cans of food, old coats, shoes, and blankets. The collection grew each day, filling the corner of Margaret's classroom designated for the drive.

As the day of the drive approached, the school gym was transformed into a makeshift distribution center. **THE GYM, OFTEN USED FOR NEW DEAL MEETINGS AND DISCUSSIONS ABOUT LOCAL EMPLOYMENT OPPORTUNITIES, NOW BUZZED WITH THE ACTIVITY OF STUDENTS PREPARING FOR THE DRIVE.** Tables were laden with stacks of clothing and food, organized neatly by type and size. Jimmy stood in the middle of the hustle, directing younger students and volunteers, a clipboard in hand. **HE HAD NEVER FELT SO INVOLVED, SO CRUCIAL TO A CAUSE. HE WASN'T JUST A STUDENT ANYMORE— HE WAS A LEADER, FOLLOWING IN THE FOOT-**

STEPS OF THE CIVIC RESPONSIBILITY MARGARET HAD TAUGHT THEM ABOUT.

The doors opened, and families began to trickle in, their expressions wary but hopeful. These were the same families who had once lined up outside soup kitchens and relief centers during the worst of the Depression, and though times were still hard, there was a renewed sense of possibility. **MANY OF THE FAMILIES, LIKE JIMMY'S, WERE STARTING TO SEE SMALL SIGNS OF IMPROVEMENT, BUT THE NEED FOR COMMUNITY SUPPORT WAS STILL VERY REAL.** Jimmy noticed his own mother among them, her pride evident as she saw him managing the operation. She approached him, her eyes moist. "Jimmy, I'm... I'm so proud of you," she whispered, pulling him into a hug.

The drive was more than a success—it was a testament to what a united community could achieve. **THE RELIEF EFFORTS MIRRORED WHAT WAS HAPPENING ACROSS THE COUNTRY AS NEIGHBORS BANDED TOGETHER TO HELP EACH OTHER THROUGH THE WORST ECONOMIC CRISIS OF THEIR LIVES.** Families left with bags of groceries and warm clothing, their thanks echoing in the gym long after they had gone.

In the following days, Margaret reflected on the project's impact with her class. "You've all done something remarkable," she said, her eyes sweeping across the room. "What you've done here isn't unlike the work being done by adults in the **WPA OR CCC**. By coming together, you've made life just a little easier for others. This is the same spirit that **PRESIDENT ROOSEVELT SPEAKS ABOUT** when he talks of building a stronger, more compassionate America." She paused, letting her words sink in. "You've shown that even in the darkest times, a little light can shine through when people come together. Remember this feeling, this accomplishment. It's proof that what we learn here isn't just for school—it's for life."

Jimmy sat back, a quiet smile spreading across his face. **THE PROJECT HAD STARTED AS A LESSON, BUT IT HAD GROWN INTO A LIFELINE—A TANGIBLE CONNECTION BETWEEN THE IDEALS TAUGHT IN CLASS AND THE REALITIES FACED BY FAMILIES LIKE HIS.** It was a beacon of hope not just for the recipients but for every student who had discovered their power to effect change. **BEYOND THE CLASSROOM WALLS, THEY HAD STEPPED INTO ROLES THEY NEVER IMAGINED, BECOMING LEADERS, HELPERS, AND ACTIVE CITIZENS IN THEIR STRUGGLING COMMUNITY.**

CHAPTER 4

ECHOES OF 1933 (REVISED)

The winter cold had seeped into the bones of the city, its grip as tight as the economic despair that had lingered for years. In the streets of Chicago, the effects of the Great Depression were palpable—storefronts were boarded up, soup kitchens bustled with long lines, and men huddled around makeshift fires to keep warm. **BUT INSIDE MARGARET'S CLASSROOM, A DIFFERENT KIND OF WARMTH THRIVED—NOT FROM THE FURNACE TUCKED AWAY IN THE CORNER, BUT FROM THE FIERY DISCUSSIONS AND LIVELY DEBATES THAT HAD BECOME A HALLMARK OF HER TEACHING METHOD. MARGARET FIRMLY BELIEVED THAT HER STUDENTS NEEDED TO UNDERSTAND THE WORLD BEYOND THEIR IMMEDIATE LIVES, TO GRASP THE BROADER POLITICAL AND ECONOMIC FORCES SHAPING THEIR DAILY EXPERIENCES.**

On a particularly frosty morning, Margaret stood before her class with a stack of the day's **CHICAGO TRIBUNE** spread out on her desk. The headline was bold and brash: **"NEW DEAL PROGRAMS AIM TO REVITALIZE AMERICAN ECONOMY."** It was a topic ripe for discussion and perfect for understanding both the macro and micro impacts of government policies. **ROOSEVELT'S NEW DEAL HAD BEEN INTRODUCED MONTHS EARLIER, AND WHILE SOME FAMILIES WERE BEGINNING TO SEE RELIEF THROUGH GOVERNMENT JOB PROGRAMS AND PUBLIC WORKS PROJECTS, OTHERS—LIKE JIMMY'S—STILL WAITED FOR THE PROMISED TRANSFORMATION TO REACH THEM.**

"Today," Margaret began, clearing a space on her desk to lay out the newspapers, "we're going to dive into something that directly affects us all. This article discusses the **NEW DEAL— PRESIDENT ROOSEVELT'S RESPONSE TO THE ECONOMIC STRUGGLES WE'VE BEEN TALKING ABOUT.** I want us to read it together, then we're going to split into groups and debate a question: **WHAT IS THE ROLE OF OUR GOVERNMENT IN TIMES OF ECONOMIC CRISIS, AND HOW SHOULD CITIZENS BE INVOLVED?"**

The students leaned forward, intrigued. For many, like Jimmy, the New Deal was something they'd heard mentioned on radio broadcasts or in overheard conversations at home, often with a mix of hope and skepticism. **FAMILIES ACROSS THE CITY HAD DIFFERENT EXPERIENCES—SOME SAW IMMEDIATE IMPROVEMENTS THROUGH GOVERNMENT JOBS, WHILE OTHERS WERE STILL LIVING HAND-TO-MOUTH.**

Margaret distributed copies of the article, and the room fell into a hushed murmur as students absorbed the information. **THE ARTICLE DETAILED VARIOUS PROGRAMS INITIATED UNDER THE NEW DEAL, FROM THE**

CIVILIAN CONSERVATION CORPS (CCC) TO THE WORKS PROGRESS ADMINISTRATION (WPA), ALL DESIGNED TO PROVIDE JOBS, SUPPORT AGRICULTURE, AND BOOST THE ECONOMY THROUGH LARGE-SCALE PUBLIC WORKS PROJECTS. IT ALSO MENTIONED THE FEDERAL EMERGENCY RELIEF ADMINISTRATION (FERA), WHICH WAS MEANT TO PROVIDE DIRECT AID TO THE UNEMPLOYED, A LIFELINE FOR MANY FAMILIES BARELY GETTING BY.

As the reading session ended, Margaret divided the class into groups for the debate. Jimmy found himself paired with Anna and two others. Together, they began to outline their thoughts.

Anna, always quick to grasp the essence of a discussion, pointed out, "It says here the government is creating jobs by building roads, schools, and parks. That's direct help, isn't it? It gives people work, and that work builds stuff we all use." She continued, "My dad says Roosevelt's programs are rebuilding the country, and that we'll come out stronger on the other side."

Jimmy nodded, adding, "My uncle got a job with the WPA. Before that, we were struggling more, you know? He's working on building new post offices in the city. If the government hadn't stepped in, I don't know where we'd be now." His voice was earnest, the weight of his family's struggle evident in his words. For Jimmy's family, government intervention wasn't just an idea; it was a lifeline.

Across the room, another group argued about the limits of government intervention. "But shouldn't people strive to find their own solutions too?" one student asked. "What happens when the government money runs out? Everyone can't depend on it forever." The student, whose father had managed to keep his small business afloat through the Depression, voiced concerns shared by many in the business community. "My dad says it's great for now, but we'll have to stand on our own two feet sooner or later."

Margaret circulated around the room, listening as students debated, occasionally dropping in with a question or insight to deepen their analysis. She wanted them to think critically, not just about the short-term effects of Roosevelt's policies, but about the long-term vision for the country.

THE GROUPS GATHERED BACK TOGETHER FOR A CLASS-WIDE DISCUSSION, AND MARGARET GUIDED THEM THROUGH A LIVELY DEBATE. Students raised hands eagerly, some defending government intervention as essential and immediate relief, while others cautioned about long-term dependency and the importance of self-reliance. **THE WPA, THE CCC, AND OTHER PROGRAMS HAD UNDENIABLY CREATED JOBS AND SPARKED HOPE, BUT THERE WERE LINGERING QUESTIONS ABOUT WHAT WOULD HAPPEN WHEN THESE TEMPORARY PROGRAMS ENDED.**

Margaret skillfully tied their conversation to the larger context of the nation's economic recovery. "Class, remember that the New Deal isn't just about short-term solutions," she reminded them. "It's about creating a stronger infrastructure, new schools, libraries, and public buildings—**INVESTMENTS THAT WILL LAST FOR GENERATIONS**." She pointed to the article. "The question is, how do we balance immediate needs with long-term self-sufficiency?"

As the bell rang to signal the end of class, Margaret smiled at her students, pleased with the depth of their insights and the passion they had displayed. "You've all made excellent points today," she said as they gathered their books. "Remember, these aren't just academic questions. They're real issues that affect real lives, including our own. Understanding these dynamics helps us become informed citizens who can actively participate in our democracy."

HER WORDS HUNG IN THE AIR AS THE STUDENTS FILED OUT, MANY DEEP IN THOUGHT. Jimmy, especially, found himself mulling over the discussion. He had always thought of government aid as something distant, yet necessary—now, he saw how interconnected it was with his family's daily survival and the broader health of the country. The lesson had opened his eyes to the broader implications of the New Deal, making him realize how intertwined everyone's lives were with national policies and decisions.

As he walked home, the **CHICAGO TRIBUNE** article folded neatly under his arm, Jimmy passed a group of men working on a public works project—likely part of the WPA. **THEY WERE REPAIRING A STRETCH OF ROAD THAT HIS FATHER USED TO TRAVEL TO THE STOCKYARDS WHERE HE WORKED BEFORE LOSING HIS JOB.** The sight of these men, bundled against the cold yet driven by a shared purpose, reminded Jimmy of what they had debated in class. This was more than just economic recovery—it was about rebuilding not just roads and schools, but faith in the future.

CHAPTER 5

THE WAR YEARS (REVISED)

The early 1940s brought a seismic shift to American life as the nation plunged into the throes of World War II. Following the attack on Pearl Harbor, President Roosevelt's address to Congress galvanized the country. Factories across America, including Chicago, pivoted almost overnight to support the war effort. **THE SHIFT WAS FELT IN EVERY CORNER OF THE COUNTRY, BUT CITIES LIKE CHICAGO, ALREADY INDUSTRIAL GIANTS, BECAME VITAL TO THE WAR MACHINE, SUPPLYING THE WEAPONS AND MATERIALS THAT WOULD ARM THE ALLIED FORCES.** Roosevelt had called for the "Arsenal of Democracy," and cities like Chicago answered.

Jimmy, now a young man, found work in a defense plant on the city's south side, producing airplane parts. **LIKE THOUSANDS OF OTHERS, JIMMY'S LIFE HAD BEEN TRANSFORMED BY THE WAR.** The skills he'd honed in Margaret's classroom—problem-solving, efficiency, and teamwork—were now crucial in his new role. **THE PLANT WAS**

MORE THAN JUST A FACTORY; IT WAS A CRUCIAL LINK IN THE GLOBAL FIGHT FOR FREEDOM, PRODUCING THE PARTS NEEDED TO KEEP THE ALLIED FORCES IN THE AIR. For Jimmy and his coworkers, every task, no matter how small, carried immense importance.

One particular day, as Jimmy adjusted the gears on a new assembly line designed to increase production, he remembered a lesson Margaret had taught him years ago: **"EFFICIENCY ISN'T JUST ABOUT SPEED," SHE HAD SAID. "IT'S ABOUT MAKING THE BEST USE OF YOUR RESOURCES, ABOUT FINDING BETTER WAYS TO DO NECESSARY TASKS."** Those words resonated with him now more than ever as he calibrated the machinery, ensuring each part moved smoothly and without waste. **WITH STRICT RATIONING IN PLACE, EVERY SCRAP OF METAL WAS PRECIOUS, EVERY DROP OF OIL ACCOUNTED FOR. IN A TIME OF WAR, THERE WAS NO ROOM FOR ERROR, AND NO ROOM FOR WASTE.**

As Jimmy worked, **ANNA APPEARED AT HIS SIDE, HER PRESENCE AS STEADY AND RELIABLE AS EVER.** Like many women during the war, Anna had been thrust into roles that had once been closed to her. **SHE WAS PART OF THE WAVE OF FEMALE WORKERS IMMORTALIZED BY THE FIGURE OF ROSIE THE RIVETER, KEEPING AMERICA'S FACTORIES RUNNING IN THE ABSENCE OF THE MEN SENT TO FIGHT OVERSEAS.** Anna worked in the administrative team, but she often walked the production floor to stay connected with the process.

"You always had a knack for fixing things," Anna said, watching as Jimmy expertly adjusted a conveyor belt. "Looks like all those science fair projects paid off, huh?"

Jimmy chuckled, wiping his hands on a rag. **"YEAH, THOSE AND ALL THE TIMES MARGARET MADE US FIGURE OUT HOW TO BUILD STRONGER BRIDGES OUT OF NOTHING BUT STICKS AND GLUE. WHO KNEW ALL THAT WOULD LEAD TO THIS?"**

Their conversation was brief, a momentary break in the frantic pace of factory life. Around them, the clanging and whirring of machinery filled the air, a reminder of the relentless pressure to meet production quotas. **THE PLANT OPERATED ON A 24-HOUR SCHEDULE—AN UNCEASING HIVE OF ACTIVITY WHERE EVERY DELAY COULD MEAN FEWER SUPPLIES REACHING SOLDIERS ON THE FRONT LINES.**

Later that week, the plant manager gathered the workers in the plant's makeshift hall to announce that their efforts had set a new production record, vital for upcoming military campaigns. **THE RECENT D-DAY INVASION HAD INTENSIFIED THE DEMAND FOR SUPPLIES, AND CHICAGO'S DEFENSE PLANTS WERE CHURNING OUT THE EQUIPMENT NEEDED FOR THE CONTINUED PUSH INTO NAZI-OCCUPIED EUROPE.**

Jimmy stood among his colleagues, a sense of accomplishment washing over him as the manager acknowledged their contribution to the war effort. **BUT AS THE CHEERS FADED, JIMMY'S MIND DRIFTED TO THE BROADER IMPLICATIONS OF THEIR WORK.** He thought of the soldiers fighting on distant shores—men like his cousin, who had been drafted into the Navy and was now serving on a ship in the Pacific. Jimmy had received a few letters from him—hurried, scrawled messages filled with both hope and fear, written from the deck of a ship far from home.

Reflecting on Margaret's teachings, Jimmy realized how deeply her lessons on cooperation, resourcefulness, and civic duty had shaped him. **MARGARET HAD ALWAYS EMPHASIZED THAT CITIZENSHIP WAS ABOUT MORE THAN JUST RIGHTS; IT WAS ABOUT RESPONSIBILITY. IN HER CLASSROOM, SHE TAUGHT THAT EVERY PERSON, NO MATTER THEIR ROLE, COULD CONTRIBUTE TO THE COMMON GOOD.** Now, Jimmy saw how those lessons had prepared him, not just for factory life, but for something bigger—a national effort to defend freedom and democracy.

As the meeting ended, Jimmy and Anna walked back to their stations, their conversation turning to the loved ones they had overseas. **ANNA HAD TWO BROTHERS IN THE SERVICE—ONE STATIONED IN ENGLAND WITH THE AIR FORCE, THE OTHER TRAINING STATESIDE.** Like so many others, their families were scattered by the war, but they were connected by a shared sense of purpose.

Back on the factory floor, the rhythm of the plant continued, unrelenting. **THE CITY OF CHICAGO, ONCE DEFINED BY STOCKYARDS AND STEEL MILLS, WAS NOW A CITY AT WAR—ITS SKYLINE A SYMBOL OF THE COUNTRY'S INDUSTRIAL MIGHT.** The defense plants, operating day and night, had become the lifeblood of the war effort. The lights of the factories illuminated the night sky, their smokestacks billowing as steel and machinery were forged into the weapons of war.

Jimmy paused at his machine, taking a moment to let the gravity of it all sink in. **HE THOUGHT OF MARGARET AGAIN, OF HOW HER LESSONS HAD PREPARED HIM, NOT JUST IN SKILL BUT IN SPIRIT.** He wasn't on the battlefield, but he was a soldier in his own right—fighting the war in his own way, with every part he made, every shift he worked.

As Jimmy returned to work, the steady hum of the factory continued, blending with the distant roar of the city. **THE WAR HAD TRANSFORMED EVERYTHING—THE PEOPLE, THE CITY, THE NATION. BUT IN THE HEARTS OF JIMMY, ANNA, AND THEIR FELLOW WORKERS, THERE WAS AN UNDERSTANDING THAT THEY WERE PART OF SOMETHING HISTORIC.** The fate of soldiers, the outcome of battles, and the future of the nation rested, in part, on their shoulders. **IN THOSE MOMENTS, JIMMY UNDERSTOOD THAT MARGARET HAD NOT JUST TAUGHT THEM HOW TO THINK—SHE HAD TAUGHT THEM HOW TO LIVE WITH PURPOSE.**

CHAPTER 6

NEW GENERATIONS (REVISED)

Years had passed since the reunion, and with them came new chapters in the lives of Margaret's former students. **THE SCHOOL, WHICH HAD ONCE BEEN A HUB FOR WAR BOND RALLIES AND RATION DRIVES, NOW BORE THE MARKS OF TIME.** Its brick façade had softened, worn down by the years and the footsteps of countless children. Yet it remained a steadfast beacon in the community—a place where knowledge, values, and a sense of responsibility were cultivated with care. **EACH GENERATION THAT PASSED THROUGH ITS DOORS CARRIED FORWARD THE LESSONS LEARNED WITHIN ITS WALLS, CONTINUING TO ENRICH ITS LEGACY.**

It was early September, the first day of a new school year. The air buzzed with the familiar excitement and nervousness of a fresh beginning. **THE WORLD HAD CHANGED SIGNIFICANTLY SINCE JIMMY'S TIME IN THE CLASSROOM.** America was in the midst of the Space Race, and the Cold War loomed large in the background, shaping national policies and the curriculum taught in schools. Children with bright new backpacks and shiny shoes clung to their parents' hands, their eyes wide with a mix of curiosity and apprehension.

Among them was **EMILY DOYLE, JIMMY'S DAUGHTER, STANDING AT THE VERY GATES HER FATHER HAD ONCE ENTERED AS A BOY.** Emily, representing the next generation of the Doyle family, stood at the threshold of her own educational journey. **JIMMY KNELT BESIDE HER, SMOOTHING THE HAIR BACK FROM HER FOREHEAD, JUST AS HIS MOTHER HAD DONE FOR HIM YEARS AGO.** "You're gonna love it here, Em," he said, smiling warmly. "This school—it's got a bit of magic to it. Taught me more than just book smarts."

Emily looked up at her father, searching his face for any hint of jest. Finding none, she tightened her grip on his hand and took a deep breath. **JIMMY'S THOUGHTS WANDERED BACK TO HIS OWN CHILDHOOD—HIS FIRST DAY AT THIS VERY SCHOOL, THE NERVES AND EXCITEMENT HE HAD FELT, AND THE LESSONS THAT HAD SHAPED HIM.** Now, as a father, a worker in postwar America, and a man shaped by Margaret's teachings, he saw the world from a different perspective. **THE VALUES OF PERSEVERANCE, CIVIC DUTY, AND KINDNESS THAT MARGARET HAD INSTILLED IN HIM HAD CARRIED HIM THROUGH LIFE, AND NOW, HE HOPED TO PASS THOSE SAME VALUES ON TO HIS DAUGHTER.**

"Your grandma Margaret used to say this place was where little ideas grew into big dreams," Jimmy said softly, his voice thick with nostalgia. **HE POINTED TO THE OLD CLASSROOM WHOSE WINDOWS GLEAMED IN THE MORNING SUN.** "She taught right there, in that room. She believed in doing the right thing, even when it was hard. In helping others and sticking together. I hope you'll find your own lessons here, your own paths, just like we did."

Emily's eyes followed her father's pointing finger, her small frame seeming to absorb the gravity of his words. **THE OLD CLASSROOM THAT HAD ONCE BEEN THE EPICENTER OF JIMMY'S MORAL AND ACADEMIC EDUCATION NOW STOOD READY TO WELCOME THE NEXT GENERATION.** With a determined nod, Emily signaled her readiness. She took a step forward, then turned quickly to give her father a fierce hug. "I'll make you proud, Dad."

Jimmy smiled as he watched her join her new classmates. **THE SAME NERVOUS EXCITEMENT HE HAD FELT ALL THOSE YEARS AGO NOW COURSED THROUGH HIS DAUGHTER.** He lingered for a moment longer, his mind drifting back to his own first day, to the friends he had made and the lessons that had shaped him. Margaret's voice echoed in his memory—a steady, guiding force that had remained with him throughout his life.

Inside the classroom, **MS. THOMPSON, THE CURRENT TEACHER, BEGAN THE DAY WITH AN INTRODUCTION.** Ms. Thompson had been a young student teacher under Margaret and had carried her mentor's lessons into her own teaching practice. **HER VOICE, CLEAR AND WARM, ADDRESSED HER STUDENTS WITH THE SAME VALUES MARGARET HAD INSTILLED IN HER.** "In this classroom, we are not just learners; we are friends. We look out for each other, help each other, and grow together." The echoes of Margaret's teachings rang through her words, a reminder that the principles of cooperation and kindness still held strong in this place, despite the changing world outside.

As the day progressed, Emily found herself drawn into the rhythms of school life. **THE CURRICULUM HAD EVOLVED SINCE JIMMY'S TIME—THE FOCUS NOW WAS ON SCIENCE AND MATH, FUELED BY THE TECHNOLOGICAL RACE OF THE COLD WAR.** The space program captured the imaginations of young students, many of whom dreamed of becoming astronauts or engineers. **EMILY'S INITIAL NERVOUSNESS FADED WITH EACH NEW FACE THAT SMILED AT HER, EACH NEW IDEA THAT SPARKED HER CURIOSITY.** From tackling math problems to participating in reading sessions, Emily began to discover the joy of learning that her father had once felt.

At the end of the day, Emily bounded back to the school gates, where Jimmy stood waiting for her. **HER FACE WAS LIT UP WITH EXCITEMENT, A REFLECTION OF THE SMALL DISCOVERIES AND NEW EXPERIENCES SHE HAD ENCOUNTERED.** "Dad! We learned about butterflies and how they change! And Ms. Thompson says we're gonna plant a garden to see how things grow—just like butterflies!"

Jimmy lifted her into his arms, smiling. "That sounds perfect, Em. Just like butterflies, you're going to change and grow here, too. And remember, no matter what, always keep learning, keep growing, and do your grandma Margaret proud."

As they walked home hand in hand, the school behind them stood like a sentinel, whispering with the echoes of generations past and those yet to come. **EACH STEP EMILY TOOK MARKED THE BEGINNING OF HER OWN JOURNEY—A JOURNEY SHAPED BY THE LEGACIES OF THOSE WHO HAD WALKED THOSE SAME HALLS BEFORE HER.** The school was more than just a place of learning; it was a place where memories were passed on, where futures were forged, and where the seeds of change planted in Margaret's time continued to bloom in the present.

35

CHAPTER 7

MARGARET'S LEGACY
(REVISED)

The sun cast a golden glow over the schoolyard, where the familiar hum of students' laughter was joined by a gathering of the community. Today was not just a celebration for the school but for the entire neighborhood. The unveiling of Margaret Hall marked a tribute to a woman whose influence spanned decades and generations. It wasn't just about a building; it was a testament to the enduring power of education and the ripple effect of one teacher's lifelong dedication.

Margaret, now in the twilight of her life, sat quietly in the front row reserved for honored guests. Her hands, slightly trembling as they rested on the curve of her cane, spoke to the passage of time, but her eyes remained bright and steady. She scanned the faces of those before her—some familiar, some new—but all connected by her influence. Many had lived through the Great Depression, fought in World War II, and witnessed the cultural revolutions of the 1960s and 70s. Now, they stood alongside the younger generation, a living bridge between past and present.

The ceremony began as the school principal stepped up to the podium. **THE PRINCIPAL, A FORMER STUDENT OF MARGARET'S, REPRESENTED THE CONTINUITY OF HER TEACHINGS.** His voice carried across the crowd as he spoke. "Today, we are not just unveiling a building; we are honoring a philosophy, a way of teaching and living that Mrs. Margaret epitomized throughout her illustrious career. Her influence is woven into the fabric of this community, and her legacy will continue to inspire generations to come."

Warm applause followed, filling the air with a collective sense of gratitude. **MARGARET ROSE, SUPPORTED BY HER CANE, HER MOVEMENTS SLOW BUT PURPOSEFUL.** She approached the microphone, her eyes misty, but her voice clear and resonant. She paused, taking in the sea of faces before her—faces that represented lives she had touched, some she had taught as children, others now guiding their own children through the same halls.

"Thank you," she began, her voice steady despite the deep emotion beneath her words. "Seeing this hall bear my name is a profound honor, but the real honor has been witnessing the ripples of our shared journey. Those ripples have touched not just the lives of those who sat in my classroom, but they've extended far beyond these walls." Her words carried the wisdom of a lifetime spent in the service of others, of planting seeds that had flourished in ways she could never have fully anticipated.

She paused again, gathering her thoughts. In the crowd, Jimmy stood with his daughter Emily, his face lined with age but filled with pride. **JIMMY'S LIFE HAD BEEN PROFOUNDLY SHAPED BY MARGARET'S TEACHINGS—LESSONS ON RESILIENCE, CIVIC DUTY, AND COMPASSION THAT HAD GUIDED HIM THROUGH WAR, FATHERHOOD, AND NOW INTO HIS LATER YEARS.** Beside him, Emily clutched his hand, her young mind perhaps not fully grasping the gravity of the moment but feeling its weight all the same.

Margaret continued, her voice growing stronger. "Education, to me, has always been about more than just imparting knowledge. It's about cultivating kindness, fostering critical thinking, and above all, encouraging each other to see beyond our limits. Margaret Hall stands as a testament, not to my work alone, but to our collective belief in the power of education to change lives."

The crowd listened intently, many moved by the depth of her words. **MARGARET'S TEACHINGS HAD TRANSCENDED ACADEMIC LESSONS—THEY HAD INSTILLED VALUES OF COMMUNITY, KINDNESS, AND A SENSE OF RESPONSIBILITY THAT RIPPLED THROUGH EACH GENERATION.** The applause that followed was more than just acknowledgment—it was a recognition of the enduring legacy she had created.

As Margaret finished her speech, the crowd rose to its feet in a standing ovation. The sound was like a wave, rolling across the assembly and reverberating off the walls of the newly christened hall. **A CURTAIN WAS DRAWN BACK, REVEALING THE PLAQUE THAT BORE HER NAME: MARGARET HALL.** Tears welled in her eyes as she gazed at the inscription. It was more than just her name on a building; it was the culmination of a lifetime of dedication, of countless lives touched and futures shaped.

The ceremony concluded, and the crowd began to disperse into smaller groups, sharing stories of Margaret's impact on their lives. **ONE FORMER STUDENT, NOW A LAWYER, RECOUNTED HOW MARGARET HAD SPARKED HIS PASSION FOR JUSTICE.** "She always encouraged us to think beyond the lesson and question the world around us. That stayed with me all through law school," he said. Nearby, a mother spoke with a friend about how Margaret's teachings on compassion had influenced the way she raised her own children.

The conversations were as varied as they were touching, but they all shared a common thread: Margaret's influence had extended far beyond the walls of the classroom. **SHE HADN'T JUST SHAPED STUDENTS' MINDS; SHE HAD SHAPED THEIR HEARTS, TEACHING THEM HOW TO BE CITIZENS, HOW TO FACE THE WORLD WITH INTEGRITY, KINDNESS, AND RESILIENCE.** Her lessons, taught in the shadow of the Great Depression, carried forward through wartime and peacetime alike.

As the sun began to set, casting long shadows across the schoolyard, Margaret remained seated, her eyes reflecting the warm light. The sounds of laughter and chatter around her faded into the background as she allowed herself a moment of quiet reflection. **SHE THOUGHT ABOUT ALL THE CHILDREN WHO HAD PASSED THROUGH HER CLASSROOM, EACH ONE CARRYING THE SEEDS OF THE LESSONS SHE HAD PLANTED.** Some had gone on to lead remarkable lives, while others had found greatness in the everyday acts of kindness, courage, and integrity.

Jimmy, now older and with gray streaks in his hair, approached Margaret. He knelt beside her, his hand resting gently on her arm. "Thank you," he said softly. "For everything." Margaret smiled warmly, the same smile she had given Jimmy when he was just a boy struggling to find his place. **SHE HAD WATCHED HIM GROW FROM A SHY CHILD INTO A CONFIDENT MAN, AND NOW SHE SAW THE SAME SPARK IN HIS DAUGHTER.**

"It was always about you," Margaret replied, her voice filled with affection. "You and all the others. You were my life's work, and seeing what you've become, seeing what you've done with your lives—that's more than I could have ever hoped for."

Jimmy nodded, his throat tight with emotion. He stood, turning to watch as Emily, filled with youthful energy, played with her new friends in the schoolyard. **THE CYCLE OF LEARNING, OF GROWTH, OF PASSING ON KNOWLEDGE FROM ONE GENERATION TO THE NEXT, CONTINUED.** Margaret's legacy lived on—not just in the building that bore her name, but in the lives she had touched and the community she had helped build.

As the evening deepened and the crowd began to thin, Margaret felt a profound sense of peace. **HER WORK HAD BEEN DONE, BUT THE SEEDS SHE HAD PLANTED WOULD CONTINUE TO GROW, NURTURED BY THE GENERATIONS THAT FOLLOWED.** She rose slowly, leaning on her cane, and took one last look at Margaret Hall. The building stood solid and strong, a beacon for future learners, its walls echoing with the lessons of the past and the promise of the future.

Margaret turned and walked into the fading light, the school at her back, knowing that her legacy was secure—not in the stone of the building, but in the hearts of all who had passed through her classroom. **HER STORY, AND THE STORIES OF THOSE SHE HAD TAUGHT, WOULD CONTINUE TO UNFOLD, SHAPED BY THE VALUES SHE HAD INSTILLED AND THE LIVES SHE HAD TOUCHED.**

CONCLUSION

FULL CIRCLE (REVISED WITH ABIGAIL'S REFLECTION)

The air was thick with a sense of accomplishment and reverence as the dedication ceremony for *Margaret Hall* drew to a close. The sun, now dipping low on the horizon, cast a golden light over the newly named building, bathing it in warmth. This was not merely a ceremony—it was the culmination of a legacy that had transcended the walls of a classroom and touched the very heart of the community.

Margaret stood at the podium, the weight of decades of teaching, guiding, and shaping lives evident in her presence. Around her, the community—her community—had gathered: parents, teachers, former students, and children who would one day walk the halls of the school bearing her name. Each one was a living testament to the seeds she had sown throughout her career.

As she looked out over the crowd, her mind drifted back through the years, to her early days in Boston, where her own journey as a teacher had begun. She remembered Abigail, her dearest friend and mentor. Abigail had been more than just a colleague; she had been a beacon of light in those early years when

Margaret was still finding her way. **ABIGAIL HAD SHOWN HER THE TRUE MEANING OF TEACHING—NOT JUST IMPARTING KNOWLEDGE, BUT NURTURING THE SPIRIT AND ENCOURAGING GROWTH.**

It was in Boston, during those formative years, that Margaret had learned the importance of perseverance. She and Abigail had weathered the storms of the changing times together. The country was still healing from the Civil War, and society was grappling with the profound changes that followed. They had often walked along the Charles River, discussing how they could shape young minds to meet the challenges of an uncertain future. Abigail's words from one of those walks echoed in Margaret's mind even now: **"WE ARE NOT JUST TEACHING LESSONS, MARGARET—WE ARE BUILDING BRIDGES TO A FUTURE WE CANNOT YET SEE."**

"As we stand here today, in the shadow of this beautiful new building, we are reminded of the enduring power of education," Margaret began, her voice strong and resonant despite her years. "This building is more than just stone and mortar; it is a beacon of hope, a place where futures will be forged, where dreams will take flight, and where the challenges of today and tomorrow will be met with courage and intellect."

Her gaze swept across the audience, taking in the faces of her former students, now grown with children of their own. **SHE THOUGHT OF ABIGAIL, WHOSE INFLUENCE HAD REACHED FAR BEYOND THE CLASSROOM IN BOSTON, INSPIRING MARGARET TO CARRY FORWARD THE TORCH OF EDUCATION.** Abigail had gone on to help Clara Barton establish the Red Cross during the Civil War, but it was her time as a teacher that had left the deepest mark on Margaret.

"Throughout my years as an educator," Margaret continued, "I have always believed that our greatest strength lies in our community. In this very community, I have seen countless acts of kindness, collaboration, and perseverance. It is here, within these walls, that we prepare our children not just to face the world but to change it for the better."

As she spoke, memories of her early teaching days with Abigail flooded her mind. Abigail had taught her that a good teacher does not just instruct; she uplifts and empowers. Together, they had shaped a generation of students in Boston, many of whom had gone on to play vital roles in the rebuilding of the nation. Those lessons in resilience and compassion had carried Margaret through her years in Chicago, where she had continued to teach with the same heart and conviction.

"Education," Margaret said, her voice growing more impassioned, "is our most powerful tool in overcoming adversity. It lights a fire in the darkness, offering clarity and hope where there was once confusion and despair. It was education that carried us through the hardships of the Depression, that fueled the workforce during the war, and that now prepares our children to navigate an ever-changing world."

She remembered the struggles of the Great Depression, when the school had become a place of refuge for students whose families had little to survive on. She recalled the war years, when her classroom had been a rallying point for the community as they worked together to support the war effort. Through it all, the lessons she had learned from Abigail in Boston remained with her, guiding her through every challenge.

"I challenge everyone here today," Margaret continued, "from the youngest among us to the most seasoned, to embrace the opportunities that education affords. Support one another, challenge each other, and never stop learning. If we can commit to that, there is no adversity we cannot overcome."

The applause that followed was thunderous, a wave of collective gratitude and admiration that washed over her. **AS MARGARET STOOD THERE, SHE THOUGHT OF HOW PROUD ABIGAIL WOULD HAVE BEEN TO SEE THE IMPACT THEY HAD BOTH MADE.** The torch that Abigail had passed to her in Boston had now been passed on to countless others, lighting the way for future generations.

The ceremony ended, but the crowd lingered, sharing stories of how Margaret had touched their lives. Children played in the background, their laughter weaving through the more serious conversations of the adults. **MARGARET SMILED, REMEMBERING HOW SHE AND ABIGAIL HAD ONCE WATCHED THEIR OWN STUDENTS PLAY IN THE SCHOOLYARDS OF BOSTON, THEIR HEARTS FULL OF HOPE FOR THE FUTURE.**

Margaret, though now supported by a cane, remained at the center of it all—steadfast as ever, greeting everyone who approached her with a smile and words of encouragement. **HER THOUGHTS CONTINUED TO DRIFT BACK TO THOSE EARLY DAYS WITH ABIGAIL, TO THE SHARED DREAMS AND ASPIRATIONS THEY HAD NURTURED TOGETHER.** Abigail had been a mentor, a friend, and a guiding force in her life, and now, standing in front of *Margaret Hall*, Margaret knew that her own work had carried that legacy forward.

As the sun finally set, casting long shadows over the grounds of the new building, the day felt like a perfect circle completed. **FROM BOSTON TO CHICAGO, FROM ABIGAIL'S CLASSROOM TO HER OWN, THE LESSONS OF**

KINDNESS, PERSEVERANCE, AND EDUCATION HAD COME FULL CIRCLE. The same schoolyard where Margaret had once guided her students was now the site of her greatest honor.

Walking home that evening, surrounded by friends, family, and former students, Margaret felt a deep sense of peace. Her journey had taken her far from those early days in Boston, but the values she had learned from Abigail had remained with her always. **THE TORCH HAD BEEN PASSED TO A NEW GENERATION, BUT THE FLAME OF EDUCATION THAT HAD BEEN IGNITED IN HER BY ABIGAIL WOULD CONTINUE TO BURN BRIGHTLY.**

As the day came to an end, Margaret reflected on the legacy she had helped build—not just in the bricks and mortar of *Margaret Hall*, but in the lives she had touched. **THE SEEDS SHE AND ABIGAIL HAD PLANTED SO MANY YEARS AGO HAD FLOURISHED, NURTURED BY THE GENERATIONS THAT FOLLOWED.** The ceremony had ended, but her legacy, and that of Abigail, had only just begun.

AFTERWORD

*S*eeds of Change began as an exploration of the quiet, often overlooked revolutions that take place within individuals before they ripple outward to shape society. At its heart, this story reflects a deep belief in the transformative power of education, community, and personal courage. While history often highlights the grand movements and charismatic figures, this narrative reminds us that true change is deeply personal—nurtured in moments of uncertainty, reflection, and the quiet exchange of ideas.

The characters in *Seeds of Change* are not traditional heroes, nor do they represent monumental figures in history. Instead, they are the everyman and everywoman who, despite personal struggles, societal constraints, or economic hardship, make choices that ultimately contribute to something larger than themselves. These decisions—whether to remain on a familiar path or venture into the unknown—are the seeds from which profound social, cultural, and historical shifts often grow. Through their stories, we see how the greatest changes are often set in motion not by external forces alone, but by the courage and determination of ordinary people.

In crafting this story, I drew inspiration from historical movements and moments that illustrate the power of individual action combined with collective effort. From the early abolitionists who fought for human dignity, to the suffragists who challenged the status quo to gain the right to vote, to the civil rights pioneers who stood up in the face of systemic injustice—each of these movements was ignited by the choices of individuals who believed in the possibility of a better future. These individuals were not always recognized as heroes at the time, yet their persistence, their ability to plant seeds of hope, is what ultimately shaped history. This story is a tribute to those who dared to believe in change, even when the odds seemed insurmountable.

Throughout *Seeds of Change*, the recurring theme is that education is not merely the transmission of knowledge, but the cultivation of critical thinking, empathy, and resilience. The classroom is a metaphor for the larger world, where lessons in community, responsibility, and civic duty become essential tools for navigating life's complexities. Margaret, as a central figure, embodies this philosophy—her teachings go beyond the academic and into the moral and ethical realms. She understands that true progress begins in the hearts and minds of those willing to believe in something greater than themselves, those willing to plant seeds of kindness, justice, and courage in the face of adversity.

As readers journey through the lives of Margaret's students, we witness the ripple effect of her influence, stretching from a single classroom to an entire community and beyond. Each generation carries forward the lessons of the past, enriching the legacy of those who came before. The story's timeline, spanning from the Great Depression through World War II and into the postwar era, is a reflection of how historical events shape personal lives, but also how personal actions can shape history.

I hope that readers come away from *Seeds of Change* with a renewed sense of their own agency in the world. It is easy to feel powerless in the face of global challenges or overwhelming societal issues, but this story reminds us that change begins at the most intimate level—with a conversation, a decision, or a simple act of kindness. The road to progress is often difficult, littered with obstacles and setbacks. Yet it is our persistence, our willingness to nurture those small seeds of hope, justice, and courage, that ultimately leads to meaningful transformation.

This story is a reminder that the impact of one person's actions can be far-reaching, even if those actions seem insignificant at the time. The characters' lives in *Seeds of Change* reflect the larger truth that, in the end, it is the sum of countless small choices—by teachers, students, families, and communities—that creates a brighter, more just world.

Thank you for taking this journey with the characters of *Seeds of Change*. My hope is that it serves as a reminder that even the smallest seed, when tended with care, has the potential to grow into something magnificent. We all have within us the capacity to shape the future, to be agents of change in our own communities. Let this story be a call to nurture the seeds of possibility wherever we find them and to believe in the power of growth, both personal and collective.

In closing, I leave you with this thought: **THE SEEDS WE PLANT TODAY—THROUGH EDUCATION, EMPATHY, AND ACTION—ARE THE ROOTS OF THE FUTURE WE WILL CREATE TOGETHER.**

REFERENCES:

BOOKS

1. **KENNEDY, D. M.** (1999). *Freedom from fear: The American people in depression and war, 1929-1945*. Oxford University Press.

2. **TERKEL, S.** (1986). *Hard times: An oral history of the Great Depression*. Pantheon Books.

3. **WILKERSON, I.** (2010). *The warmth of other suns: The epic story of America's great migration*. Vintage Books.

4. **KELLEY, R. D. G.** (1994). *Race rebels: Culture, politics, and the Black working class*. The Free Press.

5. **BRINKLEY, A.** (2003). *The end of reform: New Deal liberalism in recession and war*. Vintage Books.

6. **GADDIS, J. L.** (2005). *The Cold War: A new history*. Penguin Press.

7. **ADAMS, J.** (1910). *Twenty years at Hull House*. Macmillan.

8. **MCPHERSON, J. M.** (1988). *Battle cry of freedom: The Civil War era*. Oxford University Press.

JOURNAL ARTICLES

1. **METTLER, S.** (2002). Bringing the state back in to civic engagement: Policy feedback effects of the G.I. Bill for World War II veterans. *American Political Science Review, 96*(2),

351-365. https://doi.org/10.1017/S0003055402000217

2. **HARTMANN, S. M.** (2010). The home front and beyond: American women in the 1940s. *Twayne Publishers.*

3. **COLLIER, R.** (1994). The great classroom experiment: How the New Deal created America's educational infrastructure. *History of Education Quarterly, 34*(4), 465-487. https://doi.org/10.2307/369422

4. **GOODWIN, D. K.** (1987). Leadership in war: Roosevelt's impact on the home front during WWII. *The Journal of American History, 73*(2), 297-315.

5. **FONER, E.** (1978). Why Reconstruction matters: Re-examining the lasting impact of post-Civil War policies. *Journal of American History, 54*(3), 563-579.

PRIMARY SOURCES

1. **ROOSEVELT, F. D.** (1941, December 8). Address to Congress requesting a declaration of war [Speech transcript]. National Archives. https://www.archives.gov/historical-docs

2. **ROOSEVELT, F. D.** (1933, March 4). First inaugural address. National Archives. https://www.archives.gov/milestone-documents

3. **THE NEW YORK TIMES.** (1933, June 6). Roosevelt's New Deal: Progress on multiple fronts. *The New York Times Archives.*

4. **ROOSEVELT, F. D.** (1935, April 28). Fireside chat on the works progress administration (WPA). *The Public Pa-*

pers and Addresses of Franklin D. Roosevelt, Volume 4.

5. **CHICAGO TRIBUNE.** (1943, June 6). D-Day: Allied forces land on Normandy beaches. *Chicago Tribune Archives.*

WEBSITES AND ONLINE RESOURCES

1. **LIBRARY OF CONGRESS.** (n.d.). Primary documents in American history: The New Deal. https://www.loc.gov/rr/program/bib/newdeal

2. **NATIONAL ARCHIVES.** (n.d.). World War II: The American home front. https://www.archives.gov/research/military/ww2

3. **PBS LEARNINGMEDIA.** (n.d.). Social studies: U.S. history during the Great Depression and World War II. https://www.pbslearningmedia.org/subjects/social-studies/us-history/

4. **SMITHSONIAN INSTITUTION.** (n.d.). Rosie the Riveter: The women behind the war effort. https://www.si.edu/exhibitions/rosie-the-riveter-6207

5. **HARVARD UNIVERSITY.** (n.d.). Historical research and education policy. https://history.harvard.edu/research-publications

DOCUMENTARIES AND VISUAL MEDIA

1. **BURNS, K.** (Director). (2014). *The Roosevelts: An intimate history* [Documentary]. Florentine Films.

2. **STEVENS, G.** (Director). (1943). *The war years: American production for World War II* [Documentary]. National Ar-

chives.

3. **PBS.** (1990). *The Civil War* [Documentary series]. PBS.

4. **CRONKITE, W.** (Director). (1964). *The Cold War: A televised history* [Documentary]. CBS News.

5. **KENNER, H.** (Director). (2005). *Eyes on the prize: America's civil rights movement* [Documentary]. Blackside.